IMAGINE THAT™

Licensed exclusively to Imagine That Publishing Ltd
Tide Mill Way, Woodbridge, Suffolk, IP12 1AP, UK
www.imaginethat.com
Copyright © 2020 Imagine That Group Ltd
All rights reserved
6 8 9 7
Manufactured in China

Written by Bodhi Hunter
Illustrated by Julia Seal

ISBN 978-1-78958-588-9

A catalogue record for this book is available from the British Library

The LOUDEST ROAR!

Written by Bodhi Hunter

Illustrated by Julia Seal

The forest was full of noisy dinosaurs, but Little Tyrannosaurus (tye-RAN-uh-SAWR-us) was sure that he could make the loudest noise of all.

'I'm going to prove it!' he told Papa Rex one day, and he set off to do just that, practising his best roars as he went.

Soon, Little Tyrannosaurus found Triceratops (try-SAIR-uh-tops) who was grazing on some grass.

'Hello,' said Little Tyrannosaurus. 'Can you make a noise as loud as me?'

Triceratops let out the biggest noise that he could manage.
'BELLOW!'

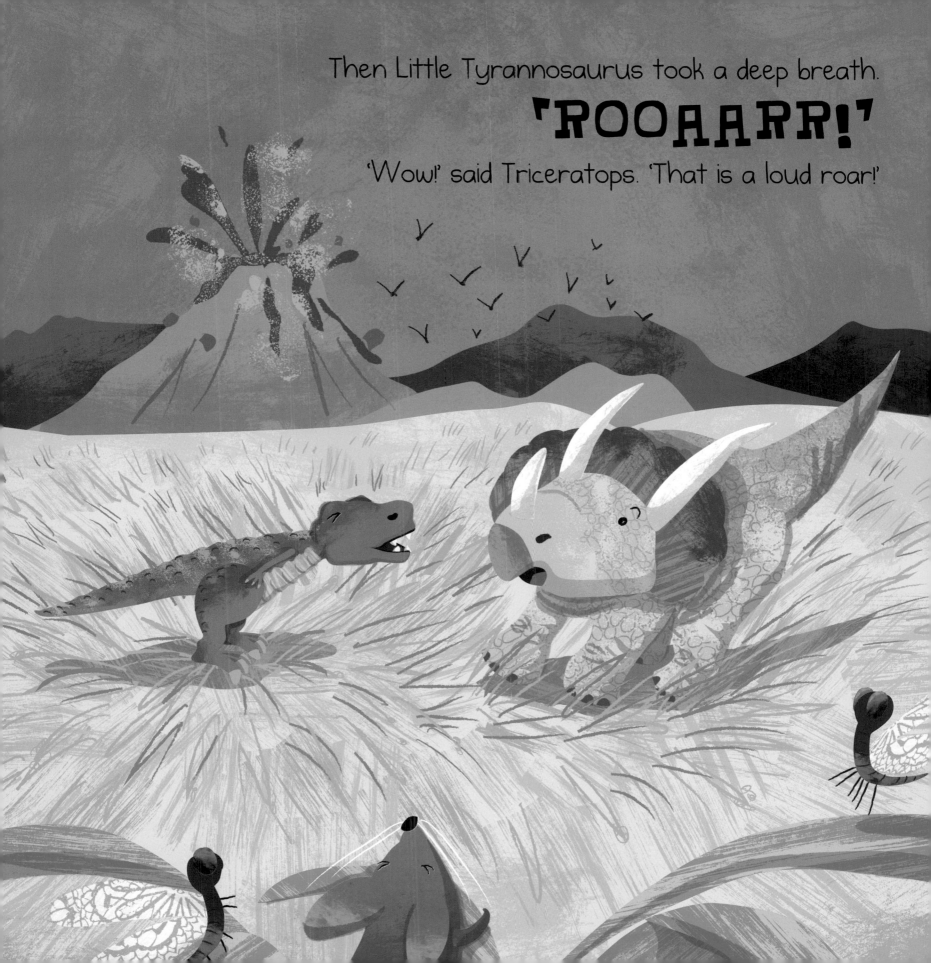

Then Little Tyrannosaurus took a deep breath.

'ROOAARR!'

'Wow!' said Triceratops. 'That is a loud roar!'

Next, Little Tyrannosaurus found Ankylosaurus (ang-KILE-uh-SAWR-us).

'Can you make a noise as loud as me?' he asked.

Ankylosaurus swished her clubbed tail as hard as she could against a tree. **'BOOM!'** went the tail.

Unimpressed, Little Tyrannosaurus roared so loudly the trees shook.
'ROOAARR!'
Ankylosaurus shook her head, 'I could never make that much noise,' she said.

Later that day, Little Tyrannosaurus spotted Diplodocus (dih-PLOD-uh-kus), munching on leaves from the tallest tree in the forest.

'Diplodocus, can you make a noise
as loud as me?' he shouted up.
'STOMP!'
went Diplodocus with his feet.

Then it was Little Tyrannosaurus' turn.

'ROOAARR!'

he roared at the top of his voice.

Diplodocus almost jumped out of his skin!

'I think you win!' Diplodocus laughed between eating mouthfuls of leaves.

Next, Little Tyrannosaurus met the raptors,
who were hunting for their dinner.

'Raptors, can you make a noise as loud as me?' he asked.

The raptors stopped what they were doing
and screeched with all of their might.
'SCREECH-SCREECH!'

It was a VERY loud noise, but Little Tyrannosaurus
let out his loudest roar so far.

"ROOAARR!"

'We can't beat that!' said the raptors.
'And you've scared away our dinner!'

Little Tyrannosaurus was very happy.
No other dinosaur in the whole forest
could make a sound as loud as him!

Then he heard a VERY big noise!
It was the loudest noise that Little
Tyrannosaurus had ever heard.

'ROOAARR!'

But where and who was
it coming from?

Little Tyrannosaurus was scared!

The VERY big noise got closer,
and closer, and closer, until finally ...

"ROAR!"

Papa Rex appeared through the trees!

'I thought I was the loudest dinosaur in the forest!'
cried Little Tyrannosaurus, 'but it's YOU, Papa! You're roarsome!'

'"ROaR!'"

"ROAR!"

"ROAR!"